Elisa Kleven

The Friendship Wish

DUTTON CHILDREN'S BOOKS
An imprint of Penguin Group (USA) Inc.

For
Mia, Maurizio, and Andreas

DUTTON CHILDREN'S BOOKS
A division of Penguin Young Readers Group
Published by the Penguin Group
Penguin Group (USA) Inc., 375 Hudson Street, New York, New York 10014, U.S.A.

Penguin Group (Canada), 90 Eglinton Avenue East, Suite 700, Toronto, Ontario M4P 2Y3, Canada
(a division of Pearson Penguin Canada Inc.) • Penguin Books Ltd, 80 Strand, London WC2R 0RL,
England • Penguin Ireland, 25 St Stephen's Green, Dublin 2, Ireland (a division of Penguin Books
Ltd) • Penguin Group (Australia), 250 Camberwell Road, Camberwell, Victoria 3124, Australia (a
division of Pearson Australia Group Pty Ltd) • Penguin Books India Pvt Ltd, 11 Community Centre,
Panchsheel Park, New Delhi - 110 017, India • Penguin Group (NZ), 67 Apollo Drive, Rosedale,
Auckland 0632, New Zealand (a division of Pearson New Zealand Ltd) • Penguin Books (South
Africa) (Pty) Ltd, 24 Sturdee Avenue, Rosebank, Johannesburg 2196, South Africa Penguin Books
Ltd, Registered Offices: 80 Strand, London WC2R 0RL, England

Published in the United States by Dutton Children's Books,
a division of Penguin Young Readers Group
345 Hudson Street, New York, New York 10014
www.penguin.com/youngreaders
Designed by Irene Vandervoort • Manufactured in China • First Edition

ISBN 978-0-525-42374-4

1 3 5 7 9 10 8 6 4 2

*F*arley bounded out into his new neighborhood, hoping to find a friend.

"Want to toss a ball?" he asked a spotted pig.

"Another time, maybe," grunted the pig. "I'm late for work."

"Can I sing along with you?" he asked a soft brown bear.

"Sorry," whispered the bear, "I need to practice."

Farley tried again. "What's up?" he called to a speckled
bird, winging by overhead.
But the bird flew on, her beak full of straw.

Everyone seems so busy, thought Farley. *I'll get busy, too.*

And he did.

But he was still lonely.
"I wish I had a friend," he said as he fell asleep.

"Me too!" someone answered.

Farley jumped up. Shimmering just overhead was an angel,
sparkly, swirly, and bright as a star, strumming a sunny guitar.

The angel fed Farley some crispy golden pancakes.

She played with him,

and sang with him,

and danced . . .

and danced with him . . .

until she danced right out of Farley's dream,

and disappeared into the quiet gray morning.

"Where did you go?" cried Farley, scampering out to find his vanished friend.

"Where did who go?" asked the speckled bird.

"My angel," said Farley. "She was just here, dancing and feeding me pancakes."

"Pancakes?" asked the spotted pig. "I love pancakes! Where did you see this nice angel?"

"In my dream," Farley replied.

The pig frowned. "Your dream! Then she wasn't real!"

"She made me really happy, though," said Farley.

"Maybe if you go back to sleep you'll see her again," said the bird.

"I'm too awake now!" said Farley. "And I feel like she's hiding, not far away."

"Who's hiding?" asked the soft brown bear.

"My angel," replied Farley.

"A *dream* angel," the pig explained, "who fed him pancakes."

"Pancakes!" The bear laughed. "I wish an angel would feed *me* pancakes."

"And the pancakes were so tasty—crisp and gold," Farley recalled.

"Maybe if you cook up some pancakes yourself, the angel will smell them and find her way back," the pig suggested.

Farley nodded. "Maybe she will!"

So Farley sizzled up some fragrant golden pancakes . . .

and set them on his picnic table.

"These pancakes are getting cold," the pig said after a
while.

"Perhaps we should eat a few," said the bird.

"You can always cook more if your angel comes back,"
the bear said hungrily.

"That's true," agreed Farley, fetching some plates.
"Dig in!" he said, and yum, the pancakes were delicious.

"What else did your angel do?" the bear asked Farley after
breakfast.

"She played with a ball, like this one," said Farley.

"And she danced with me, like this," he said.

"And she strummed a guitar and played beautiful songs. I wish I could hear my angel again."

"Well," said the bird, "maybe if we sing for your angel, she'll hear us and join in! I love to sing," she added.

"And I love to play guitar," said the bear. "Though I'm too shy to play in front of anyone else."

"Don't be shy!" said Farley. "Please play your guitar so my angel will hear!"

So they all sang together, while the bear strummed her guitar. And, wow, the sound they made was lovely, so lovely that Farley almost felt his angel were singing along with them.

Almost.

"If only I could see my angel again," Farley said.

"What does your angel look like?" the bear asked.

"She's sparkly and swirly and bright as a star," Farley explained.

The pig giggled. "Oh, I'd love to see that!"

"Me too," said the bird.

"But I don't think I'll ever find her," said Farley. "I think my angel's gone now."

"I wish we could see her," the bear said.

Farley thought for a moment. "Maybe you can," he replied.

Farley brought out his easel and paints and set to work . . .

and as he did . . . sparkle by star by sunny guitar . . .

his angel reappeared! She sparkled and swirled before them, bright as day.

Farley laughed when he saw her, and so did his friends.

And that night, they all dreamed up angels,

and brought them out to play in the morning.